THUMB AND THE
BAD GUYS

THUMB AND THE BAD GUYS

Ken Roberts

•

ILLUSTRATED BY
Leanne Franson

GROUNDWOOD BOOKS / HOUSE OF ANANSI PRESS
TORONTO   BERKELEY

To the many animals in our lives – Jake (the world's greatest mutt), Monkey (who is actually a cat), Lucky (a cat we rescued from a garbage bag in the dump), and Max (a cat we inherited). We have to include two horses who live down the street – Halloween (an energetic black thoroughbred that my daughter rides) and Tonto (the world's most serene quarterhorse).

Text copyright © 2009 by Ken Roberts
Illustrations copyright © 2009 by Leanne Franson
Published in Canada and the USA in 2009 by Groundwood Books

Groundwood Books / House of Anansi Press
110 Spadina Avenue, Suite 801, Toronto, Ontario M5V 2K4
or c/o Publishers Group West
1700 Fourth Street, Berkeley, CA 94710

We acknowledge for their financial support of our publishing program the Canada Council for the Arts, the Government of Canada through the Book Publishing Industry Development Program (BPIDP) and the Ontario Arts Council.

Library and Archives Canada Cataloguing in Publication
Roberts, Ken
Thumb and the bad guys / Ken Roberts; illustrated by
Leanne Franson.
ISBN 978-0-88899-916-0 (bound). – ISBN 978-0-88899-917-7 (pbk.)
I. Franson, Leanne II. Title.
PS8585.O2968T478 2009   jC813'.54   C2009-900286-8

Design by Michael Solomon
Printed and bound in Canada

Contents

1
Good and Evil

TAKE a deep breath. This story starts with a bang.

Here we go.

"BANG!"

"I did it," said a blonde woman dressed in a tight red gown. She held a smoking gun in one hand. Her long hair lay perfectly draped across her shoulders. Jake Danger, a private detective dressed in a tuxedo that showed no wrinkles, was lying on the floor on the other side of the room. His own blond hair wasn't quite as long, but it was just as perfect. His green eyes were riveted on the gun.

The deep blue eyes of the body next to him weren't riveted on anything. Not any more.

"You're next, Jake Danger," said the woman calmly. She cocked the trigger and held it with both hands, ready to fire.

Every eye in the gym was staring at the screen, so I reached over and stole a handful of popcorn from Susan's paper bag.

She didn't notice. I know because she didn't hit me.

"You set me up, Velma," said Jake Danger, casually wiping blood from his lip.

"I'll tell the police that I saw the two of you struggling," said Velma calmly. "I'll cry huge tears — 'boo hoo' — and say that I grabbed the gun in a panic, closed my eyes and kept pulling the trigger. I killed the burglar. Unfortunately I killed you, too. There will be tears. Lots of tears. I'm good at tears."

"I know," said Jake. "But you're forgetting one thing, Velma. I'm good at stuff, too. I'm wired, Velma. The police are listening to every word we say and you've just confessed to murder."

"Nice try, Jake," said Velma while I quietly snagged another handful of popcorn from Susan. "If you were wired the police would be kicking down the front door."

"They don't need to kick down doors," said Jake. "They're at the window."

When Velma glanced toward the living-room window, Jake Danger pulled on the runner carpet that led to the doorway where Velma stood. She started to fall, her arms waving wildly.

Jake Danger rolled behind the sofa as a shot tore through the material beside him. He pulled out his own gun, lined up the barrel with the bullet hole in the sofa and fired. He heard Velma fall.

Jake slowly stood up, his gun ready.

As soon as he saw her, Jake Danger knew that Velma Woodington, the shampoo heiress who wanted even more money than the millions she had, would be leaving her fortune to some distant relative she'd never even met.

"Greed," said Jake, slowly shaking his head. "I guess it keeps me in business."

THE END flashed across the screen and the credits began to roll.

Somebody turned on the gym lights and somebody else stopped the projector. People in the bleachers began to stand and stretch.

"Who picked that stinker?" I asked, leaning toward Susan.

"I think it was your dad," said Susan.

Exactly 143 people lived in our fishing village up the coast from Vancouver but below Prince Rupert. There were no roads to New Auckland, so every Thursday the seaplane pilot, Max, flew in three films along with the groceries people had ordered for the coming week.

There was a small cooler in the plane just big enough for four tubs of ice cream. Max always brought one tub of chocolate, one vanilla, one cherry, and one milk-free sorbet. None of the village refrigerators could keep ice cream cold enough, so all four tubs were devoured Thursday night just as the movie started. We also ate about ten pounds of popcorn.

"So, you knew it was Velma?" I asked as Susan and I walked out the door. It was spring and starting to stay light later. I could still see traces of pink in the clouds above the mountains.

"Of course I knew, silly," said Susan as we ambled along the wooden sidewalk.

"How?"

Susan shrugged. "I am a woman," she

replied softly. "Women can always tell when another woman is evil."

Susan was the same age as me, twelve. It seemed to me that she wasn't quite a woman yet but I didn't say that.

Instead I said, "You know what I don't understand?"

"I know many things you don't understand, Thumb. I probably know more about what you don't understand than you will ever understand."

"Hey, why the insult?"

Susan sighed and shook her head. "It wasn't an insult. It was a fact. Just tell me what you don't understand this time and maybe I can help."

"Okay, here's the thing. Every week at least two of the movies we watch have characters who are definitely bad guys, right?"

"What do you mean by bad guys?"

"You know, people who break the law and try to get away and don't really care if other people get hurt. Men – women – who are not very nice."

"Sure. Movies have bad guys in them."

"And none of those movies would be very interesting if there weren't bad guys, right?"

Susan thought for a moment. "Some movies aren't very interesting even with bad guys."

"Yeah, but without bad guys they'd just be movies about people taking plane rides and going to work and mowing their lawns and hugging their kids. None of us would go see them, even if there was free ice cream and popcorn and nothing much else to do most nights except count stars."

Susan laughed. "Movies aren't about real life, Thumb. They exaggerate life."

"I know. But movie bad guys are sort of good because without them we'd all be bored. I guess I'm wondering if real life can be more exciting when there are bad guys around. I mean, without bad guys, Harry Potter books would just be stories about school."

Susan stopped so I stopped, too. She folded her arms and stared at me.

"Have you always been this strange, Thumb?"

"I think so," I said seriously.

"But here's the really strange part."

"What?"

"You're starting to make sense."

I nodded. "Have you ever seen a bad person, Susan?"

"Of course not. We live in a village with mountains behind us and the ocean in front of us. We live on a beach with no roads and no bad guys."

"But good people do bad things," I said quickly. "Little Liam broke Annie's kitchen window with a rock last year."

"Yeah, but he didn't mean to. He was throwing a rock to me because he thought it was the perfect skipping rock. It was a good skipping rock, too. It was so good that it sort of curved when he threw it and broke Annie's window. But Little Liam didn't run away like a bad guy. He ran to Annie's house and knocked on the door to make sure she was all right."

"But what if there is a bad guy living here? What if some really bad person has decided that New Auckland is the perfect hiding place?

What if somebody we know and trust only lives here so that nobody from his hidden past will see him walking down a city street and turn him into the police for a huge reward?"

Susan sighed. "First," she said, holding up two fingers, "bad guys can be girls. Second," she said, holding up one finger, "wasn't hiding out in a small town the plot of one of last week's movies?"

Susan always held up the wrong number of fingers when she said a number. She started doing it as a joke, just to see if anybody would notice, but after everyone had noticed she kept doing it anyway.

We started walking again but slowly so we wouldn't reach my house before we'd finished our little argument.

"So what? It could happen. And nobody here would even think to investigate."

"Thumb? When was the last time the police set foot in our village?"

"Last year."

"Yeah. Because two policemen on vacation were fishing offshore and needed a place to stay when a storm came up."

"But they were here."

"I mean, when was the last time a policeman came here to look for evidence of some crime? I will tell you. Never."

"But don't you see? That's what would make New Auckland such a great hiding place. We don't even get television so we can't watch the news and compare pictures of wanted criminals with new people in our village."

"Thumb, almost everyone in our village was born here."

"Some people weren't born here. Like Mr. Entwhistle."

"A world-famous writer of children's books can't really hide, you know? What about your dad? He's only been here about four years."

"You're right," I said excitedly. "Maybe I'm the son of a bad guy and when I discover the secret of Dad's hidden past I will have to fight an inner struggle between loyalty to family and knowledge of my father's past cruelty."

Susan stopped and looked at me. She rolled her eyes.

"Wasn't that the plot of a movie we saw last month?"

"Susan, I just think that maybe we should make sure our village really is safe from evil."

"Us?"

"Why not?"

"Because nothing ever happens here, Thumb!"

"I know. But wouldn't our lives be a little less boring if we spent just a little time looking for a bad guy? Sure, we know that nothing ever happens during the daytime. But what about at night?"

"Night?"

"Most criminals work at night, right?" I asked excitedly. "So if anybody here is doing bad-guy stuff then they probably work at night."

I stopped and thought for a moment and then whispered, "We need to stake out the village."

"Stake out this village? Nobody even jaywalks here."

"That's because there aren't any streets."

"Well, nobody would jaywalk if there were streets. We know everybody here. We know their favorite colors and their hobbies and what books they have on their shelves. There are no bad guys living in New Auckland, Thumb."

I smiled.

"Maybe not," I said. "But even the possible existence of one single bad guy could be a little exciting, right? We could stay out late and watch the village for a couple of nights, couldn't we? We could be sneaky but in a good way since we'd be crime fighters. We'd have a secret that nobody else would know."

"A secret?" asked Susan.

I knew she liked secrets.

"Our secret," I said softly, making sure that nobody else could hear.

"Our secret," said Susan, more to herself than to me.

"Tomorrow night? Ten o'clock?"

"Why wait?"

"Tonight is a school night."

"I'll meet you by the fire truck," said Susan, her eyes glancing around to make sure nobody else could hear. "At dusk."

2

Stakeout

IT'S hard to sneak out of a house that only has four rooms — two bedrooms, a living room/ kitchen and a bathroom. It's even harder when only the bathroom has walls that go all the way to the ceiling. It's harder still when you share the house with your dad and he's the principal of the school so he stays up most nights grading papers and filling out reports.

I knew I could fit through my bedroom window, but I also knew that trying to sneak out the window would make a lot of noise.

It would be easier on a Friday night. Dad didn't grade papers on Fridays because Mayor Semanov usually came over to talk politics. Mayor Semanov was our mayor when we needed one. He was mayor mostly because he had a loud voice.

We held all village meetings in the school

gym. There was a microphone and an amplifier up at the school, but it hissed and popped and tended to amplify almost every sound except for voices. It was easier to make Big Charlie Semanov our mayor than it was to fix the school's sound system.

Big Charlie liked to make speeches even when he was just sitting around and talking with Dad. I knew that once he started a speech I could crawl out the window and Dad wouldn't hear.

After dinner Mayor Semanov did come over. He wanted to talk about Miss Mitchell, the teacher who had left on Thursday's seaplane. Miss Mitchell had been the teacher for the older grades. She was a city woman who came to New Auckland because she said she wanted to live close to nature.

It hardly ever snows in New Auckland and even when it does, the snow melts by noon. But the wind from the ocean can work its way through the fabric of any coat and the walls of any house.

After a winter in New Auckland, Miss

Mitchell decided to keep nature at a more respectful distance.

Yesterday, Max the pilot and a couple of fishermen unloaded our groceries from the seaplane and set them on the dock. Just as Max started to climb back inside his plane, Miss Mitchell ran out of the teacher's house where she'd been living. She was rolling two huge suitcases along the wooden sidewalk behind her and they clanked as the wheels hit the gaps between each board. As she ran, she yelled for Max to wait.

As soon as Miss Mitchell stopped next to the seaplane Big Charlie, our mayor, politely tossed her suitcases onto the back seat. Miss Mitchell caught her breath, nodded a thank-you and scrambled into the plane.

Everyone on the dock just waved. They knew she was leaving for good and there was nothing much to do except smile and say good luck.

Teachers and visitors often left New Auckland suddenly. People left for lots of reasons.

One evening some fishermen from Florida

arrived at our dock and asked if we had a vacant house they could use for a week. We did but they left after one night. They said they just couldn't sleep knowing the mountain behind the village could drop boulders on their heads.

I don't know how people can be so afraid of boulders falling when they live next to streets where cars speed by and airplanes fly over your house. I suppose it's just a matter of being comfortable with what you know.

The night before they left, one of those fishermen told us about swimming in a Florida spring that flows into the St. Johns River. The spring water was cool and crystal clear and when you were underwater you could see alligators in the warmer river waters a hundred yards away. The spring water was too cold for those gators so they just licked their toothy lips and stared longingly at all the swimmers splashing and yelling and having fun.

"Weren't you scared?" I asked the guy from Florida who told us about swimming so close to gators.

"No," he said, laughing. "You get used to it.

Reptiles can't swim into cold water. They just can't do it."

I thought he was so brave but he left the village the next morning, shaking and staring bug-eyed at the mountains like they were haunted.

The only mountains in Florida are in amusement parks.

Sitting in our living room, Dad was calmly telling Big Charlie that the school board had already hired another teacher and she was coming soon, maybe even that weekend. We needed another teacher fast. There were only two teachers at the school, including Dad.

I wanted Big Charlie to start talking loudly to mask the sound of me slipping through the window, so I said goodnight and then casually mentioned that I'd heard on the radio that the federal government might reduce fishing quotas for salmon. I knew that government decisions about fishing quotas made Big Charlie mad, and when he was mad his voice could shake the walls of our house.

It worked, of course. I covered the pillows

on my bed with sheets so they looked like me and was out the window and sneaking toward the fire truck in less than a minute.

Susan was late.

"Sorry," she said when she finally arrived.

"What took you so long?"

"Mom always goes to bed early but Dad only goes to bed early when he plans on fishing early. Tonight he wanted us all to sit around and talk."

"So, how did you escape?"

"It was easy. Your dad and Big Charlie came over, all upset. Big Charlie heard that fishing quotas might be reduced. He wants to start a petition."

I laughed.

"Shh," said Susan. "I don't think we should be laughing on a stakeout."

"You're right. Let's hide inside the fire truck."

Last year, after a small fire in a shed which we put out with a bucket brigade, Big Charlie asked the federal government for a saltwater pump. Our federal Member of Parliament, who

was up for re-election, wrote back and said that he could arrange for the government to send us a used fire truck. We reminded our MP that there were no roads in New Auckland, but we got a fire truck anyway. We took out the pump and used the truck as a huge piece of playground equipment.

The fire truck sat on the sand halfway between the school and the houses in our village. New Auckland was tucked into a large bay with a narrow entrance, and we actually faced away from the ocean with a huge mountain behind us. All of the houses in our village were lined up in two rows that faced the beach.

Susan climbed behind the steering wheel, and I sat beside her. A light breeze swept through the cab.

"Dad told Big Charlie that we're getting another teacher soon," I whispered. "Maybe even this weekend."

"Good," she said. And then she asked, "If there is a bad guy in our village, do you have any suspects?"

I liked the word suspect.

"Do you?"

"I asked first."

I paused.

"I know that really bad guys can be fake nice and pretend to be your friend," I said.

"How do you know that, Thumb?"

"Movies."

"So you don't know anything, right?"

"Look, it doesn't make any difference. I have my suspect."

"Who?"

"Kirk McKenna," I said quietly.

Kirk McKenna was a toothless, bald fisherman who was always borrowing Annie Pritchard's boat because his own broke down so often. He only weighed about 130 pounds, most of it skin that seemed to hang from his arms and legs and belly and even his ears.

"Why?" asked Susan.

"He spits," I said.

Susan's eyes narrowed. She knew I was right. Kirk McKenna was always spitting. During Thursday night movies he didn't even sit in the stands. He stood beside the gym door and kept turning his head so he could spit outside.

No plants grew close to that door.

When Kirk McKenna walked along the cedar sidewalk that ran in front of all the houses in our village, he didn't turn his head and spit onto the sand. Instead, he spat three feet in front of him.

It rains a lot in New Auckland, and the cedar sidewalk was usually wet from the rain or fog or just the damp ocean air. But even though the sidewalk was almost always wet, you could still see a stain every place Kirk McKenna's spit had landed. Each drop looked like a tiny oil slick. Dad figured that every inch of that sidewalk would eventually be soaked with Kirk McKenna's spit.

"So we're waiting to see if Mr. McKenna is a bad guy because he spits?"

"A lot. He spits a lot. And if Kirk McKenna cared about people then he'd at least turn his head and spit on the sand."

"Good point."

People started turning off their lights. We saw Dad and Mayor Semanov and Susan's dad step out of her house. They all shook hands and said goodnight.

I was a little nervous, wondering if Dad might check on me before he went to bed. He didn't, though. A few minutes after he got home, the lights in our house went out, too.

I was used to seeing lots of stars but was surprised to see that the number of stars seemed to double when the village was dark. The mountains around us were visible mostly because they weren't visible at all. They were black shapes where no stars could be seen.

"Next time let's bring a blanket," I said.

"You think there's going to be a next time?"

"Aren't you having fun?"

"Well, I can only say that sitting here in the dark when I could be sleeping is making me wonder why staking out the village seemed like such a good way to fight boredom, especially when − "

"Shh," I said.

"What?"

"I see a shadow moving between the houses. It's coming this way."

Susan and I both ducked lower so we couldn't be seen. I heard the gentle lap of waves slapping the beach and the sound of boat hulls nudging against the dock. I also heard the sound of a person trudging through the sand, heading right toward us.

Susan heard it, too. She grabbed my hand and held it tightly. The person stopped right beside the fire truck.

And then I heard a sound I recognized because I had heard it so many times before.

Somebody, leaning against the fire truck and looking back at the village, spat.

3

A Secret Hiding Place

SUSAN and I huddled together and listened. She wasn't bored any more. She was scared.

Kirk McKenna hummed a tuneless song while he tapped his fingers on the fire truck. When the song was finished, he spat one last time before walking behind the school.

We knew where he was heading. Only one trail left the village. It sneaked through boulders behind the school and then slowly climbed Linda Evers Mountain. Five minutes up the trail there was a large pond on a small plateau.

The pond was created by a clear mountain stream that flowed into it and then back out, before cascading into the ocean not far from our village. The pond was about the size of a little league baseball diamond, and it was very deep and very clean. It was one of the main reasons we had a village. We piped fresh water from it down to our houses.

We sent water samples out with Max the pilot about once a month. We'd never had any problems with the water except for one time when a family of beavers decided that our pond would make a good home. We never did figure out how those beavers knew that if they climbed halfway up a mountain they'd find a place to live. Maybe beavers can smell fresh water. Or maybe there were beavers wandering over all our mountains, searching for places to settle.

Last year, Mayor Semanov trapped five beavers and put them in his fishing boat and dropped them off at a cove up the coast. A month later we had beavers again. I think it was the same ones. Our mayor trapped them a second time and dropped them at an island down the coast. This time they didn't come back.

The trail behind the school didn't stop at the pond. It continued higher still, climbing over rocks and around big boulders. It stopped at a hump on the side of Linda Evers Mountain where you could stand and see the entire ocean, no mountains in the way. The flat hump was called Black Bear Hump because a black bear was once spotted there. I think he liked the view.

Sometimes Dad and I climbed the trail to Black Bear Hump at sunset. There's an old gnarled cedar and we'd sit with our backs against it and watch the orange sun seem to settle right into the ocean.

I've stood at Black Bear Hump and seen fishing boats and oil tankers and cruise ships glide down the coast from Alaska, and every time I saw a cruise ship I knew that hundreds of eyes were probably staring at me. I knew that people on those ships couldn't tell there was a small village tucked into a bay behind the mountains, unless they saw smoke on a clear winter morning.

Susan and I slipped out of the fire truck. We could see Kirk McKenna's shadow as he followed the beam of his flashlight behind the large boulder that masked the trail up to our pond. We raced across the sand to the bottom of the trail. We listened for a moment and then — without even discussing what we should do — we both started to climb.

We didn't have to worry about making noise. We mostly stepped over large flat granite rocks that twisted around boulders. Susan and I knew every turn. Kirk McKenna's constant humming let us know that he was still going up and not listening for somebody following him.

"What if he turns and starts coming back down?" whispered Susan.

"We'll just slip off the trail," I said with more confidence than I actually felt.

"But what if he really is a bad guy and he discovers that we're spying on him?"

"Kind of exciting, isn't it?" I asked with a grin.

I wasn't sure if she saw my grin since it was dark.

"I'd feel better if we let him have a little more lead," said Susan.

We waited. I could see the flashlight beam vanish as Kirk McKenna reached the pond. We couldn't hear him humming any more so we just stood there staring at the dark, quiet mountain above us.

"You didn't think we'd see anything on our stakeout, did you?" I asked.

"No."

"You just thought it might be fun to pretend we were spies, right?"

"Yeah."

"Scared?"

"Sure. When we get close to the top he might be right in front of us, waiting. We don't know where he is right now."

We climbed more slowly, stopping to listen after every few steps.

As we sneaked closer, I could hear the mountain stream rushing down to our pond and flowing out again to the ocean below. The sound of water was so loud that I was sure Kirk McKenna couldn't possibly hear us. I was just as sure we couldn't hear him, either, even if he was close.

Susan and I reached the last big boulder before the plateau. We knew that the pond was on the other side. I pressed my back against the cold granite and slowly peeked around the corner. I couldn't see any flashlight beam and couldn't see any shadows that moved. I pulled my head back and stood next to Susan, breathing deeply.

"What did you see?" she asked quietly.

"Nothing. It's too dark."

"What happens now? I don't want to get any closer. He might be waiting for us."

"If we climb a boulder we can hide on top and still see his flashlight beam whenever he comes back."

"Do you think he went up to Black Bear Hump?"

"I don't know. I just know I can't see him."

Susan nodded and we climbed to the top of a boulder and hid behind some large rocks. Unless we moved or stood up, nobody would be able to tell we were there.

I watched and listened.

Susan grabbed my arm and whispered, "Listen."

Over the roar of the water I could just hear a distant painful wail, like a person being tortured in the movies.

"What is that noise?" asked Susan.

"Wolves?"

"No. It's too creepy." She shivered.

The noise would stop for a few minutes and then start again. It didn't get louder or closer but it stayed creepy and strange, like fingernails on a blackboard but changing pitch and tone.

It finally stopped, but I didn't know if that was a good sign or a bad one.

I could hear Susan breathing. I glanced over at her.

"Susan," I said quietly.

"Yeah?"

"I see a light."

We ducked even lower. Susan glanced toward the pond. Light seemed to come from inside the waterfall that cascaded down from our pond to the small stream below it. The light got brighter and then disappeared for a few seconds before it reappeared, shining toward us. The light jiggled around as Kirk McKenna made his way from rock to rock and back up to the path.

Kirk McKenna stopped right below us and shone the flashlight back toward the way he'd

come. He spat and then walked slowly toward something he'd spotted. He bent down low and roughed up a bit of soil with his fingers.

"He's hiding his footprints," I whispered to Susan.

"There just might be a bad guy in our village," Susan said softly. I could hear the tremor in her voice. "What are we going to do, Thumb?"

"We're going to stay right here until Kirk McKenna is back inside his house and snuggled up in bed."

"And then?"

"And then we'll sneak back down and after a good night's sleep we're going to find out why Kirk McKenna wiped away his footprints."

"I don't think I'll be sleeping much," said Susan, ducking down to make sure Kirk McKenna had no chance of spotting us.

I ducked, too.

We'd seen enough.

4

Ms. Weatherly

S USAN didn't want to look for some hidden
path below the pond unless Kirk McKenna
was out fishing. He didn't go anywhere on
Saturday, so Susan and I hung around the dock,
helping to mend nets and keeping an eye on his
house.

Kirk McKenna didn't fish on Sunday, either,
but just after lunch the seaplane, which usually
came only on Thursdays, swooped between
mountains and circled the village. We knew that
Max had a passenger because he only circled
when he was giving somebody the chance to
look down at the village and to peek behind
mountains before landing.

Max landed on the flat waters of the bay
and his plane glided slowly toward the dock.
Susan and I each grabbed a line and hopped
onto the nearest pontoon. We pulled the

seaplane tight to the dock and then tied off the lines.

Max opened the door to the cockpit. He climbed down and then reached inside and pulled out a couple of suitcases.

His passenger, a woman, climbed out backwards and carefully stepped first onto the pontoon and then onto the dock. She was slender and tall and had tight blonde curls that looked plastered to her skull.

She turned around and looked over at me, and I tried hard not to gasp.

She wore so much make-up that when she smiled, the smooth surface of her face cracked like dried mud. Her lipstick was bright red and it covered more than just her lips. Her cheeks had perfectly round circles of pink rouge, and her eyebrows looked too long and too thick to be real. She wore a loose dress with a pattern on it that looked like wallpaper – bright red with large yellow flowers blooming everywhere. The curls on her head were not made of hair at all but of nylon sparsely attached to what looked like a white bathing cap.

"I've brought the new teacher," said Max to me, smiling. "Could you and Susan carry her bags up to the house?"

"The new teacher?" asked Susan, almost in a whisper.

"Ms. Weatherly," said the woman, nodding to us.

"My name is Thumb," I said. "And this is Susan."

"Thumb?"

"It's kind of a nickname. I lost my thumb in an accident. My real name is Leon Mazzai but I haven't heard that name used out loud for so long that it sounds like it belongs to a distant relative, not me."

"I can see both thumbs, young man. Did they sew your thumb back in place?"

"Nope." I held up my right hand and wiggled my thumb. "This one is a fake. I can take it off. I have to take it off sometimes, just to clean it."

"Oh," said Ms. Weatherly.

I didn't really have a fake thumb. But I did have a beautiful cedar box that Annie Pritchard had carved. The box had a hole in the bottom so my real, attached thumb could poke through and rest on a bed of cotton and look like it was just lying there. When visitors came to the village we all tried to convince them that my thumb was a fake so we could get them to peer into the box. Then, when they were inspecting my thumb, I'd wiggle it and scare them.

I know it sounds silly. I guess we liked to think that we knew something that people who lived in cities didn't know. We had a secret, a joke that made us feel good when sophisticated city folk fell for it.

Susan and I carried Ms. Weatherly's bags up to the vacant house where the teacher lived. It looked just like every other house in our village. Teachers didn't have to pay rent. It was one advantage of teaching in New Auckland and was probably the only way we ever managed to get teachers.

As soon as we showed Ms. Weatherly her house, I ran to tell Dad that she had arrived. Dad dropped the book he was reading, put on a clean shirt and rushed off to introduce himself and to invite the new teacher to dinner.

5

Message from the Past

I WOKE up early on Monday and ran to Susan's house.

Dad and I lived in the middle of the row of houses closest to the bay. Susan lived in the second row. She didn't have the same view, but at least the wind didn't whistle through every crack in the house. Sometimes the wind was so strong inside our place that we had a hard time keeping a match lit when we wanted to light a fire.

I waited for Susan on the cedar sidewalk. I think it was raining. Sometimes the rain that fell on New Auckland was more like a heavy mist or a damp fog.

I was wearing a baseball cap. Tiny drops of water hung from the edge of the cap, suspended for long seconds before falling.

I could hear the whine of outboard motors

as kids from smaller villages arrived for school.

"Maybe Ms. Weatherly is a bad guy," I blurted out even before Susan had completely opened her front door.

"What?"

"She came to dinner at our house and Dad asked why she wanted to come to a place like New Auckland."

"What did she say?"

"Well, that's just it," I said as we started walking to school. "She didn't say anything. She kept changing the subject."

Our new teacher was writing her name on the chalkboard when we got to the classroom. Her back was turned to us. She wore a bright green dress with purple flowers on it.

Nobody was late, and when the bell rang, Ms. Weatherly turned around and said, "Good morning, class."

I gasped. If anything, she was wearing even more make-up than she'd worn when she got off the plane and came to our house for dinner. She wore so much make-up, I was surprised she could hold her head up.

"Good morning," I heard myself and others say back.

"My name is Emma Weatherly but you can call me Ms. Weatherly. I am your teacher for the rest of this year."

She sighed, like she was surprised and almost sorry to have heard her own words. Her eyes darted to the side window where she couldn't see much, mostly the side of a mountain and a few scattered boulders in the sand. There were some small shrubs and trees that were struggling to survive in niches they'd found. Unlike animals or people, they couldn't pack up and travel to a place where life might be easier.

"I like projects," said Ms. Weatherly. "It is my belief that kids learn when they are excited about projects. Grab your coats and follow me."

We all stood up. Ms. Weatherly made her way to the back of the classroom and then led us down the short hallway.

As soon as she was outside, she raised an umbrella over her head and walked toward the village. We followed, of course.

I had never seen anyone use an umbrella in New Auckland. When it rained, everyone wore hats or just let rain fall on their heads. Umbrellas were something that women in movies about life in another century used to shield themselves from the sun while they lounged in skiffs rowed by young men with English accents.

We stopped in front of Mayor Semanov's house.

All of the houses in New Auckland had very small front yards. Each front yard was divided by a narrow cedar walkway that led up to the front door. Nobody had grass or flowers. I don't think plants could grow in our sand.

Some people had a few large rocks that they painted different colors and laid out in patterns. Others had small headstones to remind them of relatives who had died. None of the relatives were buried in the village. They were buried on an island down the coast.

Mayor Semanov had something different sitting in his front yard. He had a big iron ball. It looked like one of those balls that cartoon convicts wear shackled to their ankles, except it was rusted.

Ms. Weatherly pointed to Major Semanov's iron ball and said, "Class, what is that?"

"It's an iron ball," I said.

"Yes. It is," said Ms. Weatherly.

I grinned.

"What else?"

We all looked at each other. Nobody said anything.

"Did anyone in this village ever ask the man who owns this house where he found this very interesting ball?"

I knew that Big Charlie Semanov had found his iron ball on the shore near the narrow entrance to our bay. He had lost some buoys and spotted them washed onto the rocks. He rowed a dinghy to shore and found that iron ball wedged between two rocks. He hefted the iron ball over to his dinghy and carefully placed it between struts and surrounded it with buoys so it wouldn't roll around. Then he brought it back to New Auckland and dropped it in the sand in front of his house as decoration.

Everybody noticed it, of course, and we all thought it was an odd thing to find on a beach. It couldn't have washed on shore. It was too heavy. Somebody must have put it there.

We all knew the story of how Big Charlie had found that scrap of metal but none of us said a word. We just weren't used to telling teachers about things that happened in our village.

We all looked at each other again and shook our heads.

"All right. Back to class."

We marched back into the school, stopping only to let Ms. Weatherly close up her umbrella before stepping inside.

We sat down in our seats.

"Any ideas about the original purpose of that iron ball?" asked Ms. Weatherly.

"It looks like something a convict would wear," I suggested.

Ms. Weatherly laughed. "Good idea, but unless there's a loop for the shackle, not possible."

"I always thought it was some piece of antique fishing equipment," said Susan. "Something to keep a net from floating to the surface."

"Good thought," said Ms. Weatherly, "but far from the truth."

"So, you know what it is?" asked Big Bette, the smallest person in our class, even though she was in grade seven, just like me.

"I do indeed."

Before we could ask about that iron ball beside Mayor Semanov's front door, something truly strange and astonishing happened.

One of the blonde curls on Ms. Weatherly's head fell to the floor.

I don't mean a strand or two of hair fell to the floor. I mean that a complete curl, composed of hundreds of strands of genuine man-made nylon, drifted down to the floor, bounced twice, flipping each time, and then came to a rest next to Ms. Weatherly's left foot.

Nobody laughed. We all just stared down at that curl.

Ms. Weatherly stepped away from it, causing all of us to look up at her.

We gasped. We could see where the curl belonged because Ms. Weatherly now had a curl-sized patch of white plastic on the side of her head.

Ms. Weatherly sighed and calmly walked to her desk. She opened her top drawer, reached inside and pulled out a container of white glue. Holding the glue in one hand, she walked back to the curl and picked it up.

"Any other ideas?" she asked as she casually squeezed some glue onto the curl. She set the glue bottle on her desk before rubbing the glue around one side of the curl and then gently lifting it to the bare white patch on her cap and holding it in place. She kept holding it as she looked at each one of us, waiting for someone to answer her question.

"Let's go back and look at that iron ball one more time," said Ms. Weatherly, letting go of her curl. It stayed in place, as she seemed to know it would. She picked up her umbrella and led us back outside.

Five minutes later we all stood in front of Mayor Semanov's house again, staring down at the iron ball.

To understand what happened next, you need to know that when good fishermen from any country in the world wake up, they all look at the ocean or the river or the lake or pond where they plan to fish.

Fishermen in New Auckland gaze at our bay every morning, as soon as they get out of bed. They look out a window before they go to the bathroom or turn on the kettle or put the dog out. It doesn't have to be a long look. With just a quick glance any good fisherman can read the color of the water or the rhythm of the swells.

One summer a fellow from a university came and stayed in our village for a week. He was a bug specialist who identified eight species of hoverflies within minutes of hopping out of the seaplane.

Fishermen are like that man. They learn how to look for things most of us simply ignore and treat as background scenery.

Big Charlie Semanov hadn't planned to fish that morning, so he'd slept late and when he looked out his window he didn't see the ocean at all. Instead, he saw an entire class of kids and one quite strange-looking woman with an umbrella all standing in front of his window, staring down.

Big Charlie quickly opened his door so that

he could look down, too, in case there was something wrong with his house. He didn't see anything unusual.

"What are you all doing here?" asked Big Charlie.

"We were just looking at your cannonball," said Ms. Weatherly.

"My what?"

"His what?" asked eighteen kids.

"Your cannonball. On the ground right here. Where did you get it? It's quite a find."

"You mean that round metal thing?"

"Yes."

"How do you know it's a cannonball?"

"Well," said Ms. Weatherly, sticking her hand out from under her umbrella. Her fingers came back dry so she folded up her umbrella and tucked it under one arm. "I spent the early years of my life in museums, staring at cannonballs and swords and muskets. My mother was responsible for a museum and I used to roam the hallways when she worked late. This is a cannonball. It is British, and it is eighteenth-century. You found it up here someplace?"

"Yes."

"Then there's a good chance that it came here with Captain James Cook, who explored and claimed this coast for England. If you had found this cannonball in the Caribbean or the Mediterranean then we would never be able to guess its history. But the only eighteenth-century explorers in this area were Captain Cook, George Vancouver and George Dixon. Where did you find it?"

"On the beach by the narrows," said Big Charlie.

Ms. Weatherly kneeled down and took a long, close look at the cannonball. She stood up again and pointed at it.

"This cannonball has never been fired."

"How can you tell?"

"A cannonball can't simply explode out of a barrel without scraping the sides. There are no scrape marks."

"What does that mean?"

"I have no idea. I can only tell you that it wasn't fired from a cannon. How did it get on that beach?"

"Well, it sure didn't roll there," muttered Mayor Semanov.

Ms. Weatherly turned to all of us and said, "Back to class. We have a mystery to solve." Then she turned and started marching back toward our school, almost dragging the rest of us behind her.

"Take your seats," she said when we were back inside. "Quickly. Quickly."

"We have us a puzzle," said Ms. Weatherly when we were settled. "We have a cannonball from the past. Let's see if it has any secrets to tell."

"I don't think metal balls can talk," said Little Liam seriously, which was actually pretty interesting because for entire months at a time most of us weren't sure if Little Liam could talk.

"But it can tell secrets," said Ms. Weatherly mysteriously, almost like she was trying to keep a secret herself.

I sat back, trying to make a tough choice.

Dad insisted that I tell him one story and only one story at the end of every day. It had to be a story about something interesting that I had learned or heard or saw or thought. Some days it was a challenge to find that one single story, but on Ms. Weatherly's first day of school, I had choices.

I could tell Dad about the nylon curl floating to the floor and Ms. Weatherly gluing it back almost in the right place. Or I could tell him that Big Charlie Semanov had an eighteenth-century cannonball in his front yard.

"I am going to divide you into teams," said Ms. Weatherly. "Who would like to read about the voyages of Captain James Cook and the other explorers and try to see when any of them might have explored along here?"

Robbie and Big Bette raised their hands. I wasn't surprised that Robbie volunteered. Robbie was great with computers and loved those role-playing games where you pretend to be on an expedition or a crusade.

"If you can," added Ms. Weatherly, "try to find out what kinds of cannons they had on their ships."

Robbie and Big Bette nodded.

"Who would like to take pictures of that cannonball, with your mayor's permission, of course, and try to see if there are any markings? You'll have to weigh it, too, and read all you can about cannonballs."

Little Liam raised his hand. Nick, too.

"And finally," said Ms. Weatherly, "who would like to explore the rocky beach where the cannonball was found? Look around. If you do find something, leave it in place so the whole class can have a look. Who knows? Maybe a ship sank on the rocks and there are lots of artifacts."

Susan and I glanced at each other, nodded and then raised our hands.

"Excellent," said Ms. Weatherly.

"Look," said Susan, whispering out of the side of her mouth and looking at me. "Down at the dock."

I glanced out the window beside the blackboard. Five fishing boats rested next to the dock. Men were loading nets and supplies. One of the five boats belonged to Kirk McKenna.

We watched him untie the back line on his boat and toss it on deck. Then he untied the front line and, holding it, jumped on board. He fired his engines and slowly made his way toward the narrow mouth of the bay.

Kirk McKenna was going fishing.

6
A Clue

AFTER school, Susan and I met behind the boulder that guarded the path up to the pond.

"I don't think anybody saw me," I said.

"Me, either," said Susan quietly.

We both ran up to the spot just below the pond where Kirk McKenna had bent over and erased a footprint.

I crouched down like I'd seen trackers do in Western movies and ran my hands over the dirt. I had no idea what I was trying so hard to find.

"He definitely came from below the pond," I said.

We jumped from rock to rock and stopped next to the waterfall by the stream below the pond. The waterfall wasn't wide and most of the far side was lined with boulders so big that you couldn't see past them.

I stood beside the stream, staring.

"Don't even think about trying to swim or wade over," said Susan firmly. "You could get killed."

"Kirk McKenna was over there."

"Maybe our eyes were playing tricks on us. There's no way to cross."

"What if I go under the waterfall?" I asked as calmly as possible.

"Are you crazy?"

"No. We saw a flashlight beam that seemed to almost glow, like it was shining through water. Maybe when the water falls down from the pond it leaves a dry space behind it, like a cave. Maybe I can walk through that space to the other side."

"You've been watching too many movies, Thumb."

"If I'm right I should be able to put my hand right through the water near the edge here and feel air on the other side."

I held onto a rock next to me while Susan grabbed the back of my sweatshirt. I plunged my hand into the waterfall.

I pulled my hand back out, turned to Susan and grinned.

"I'm going through," I said.

I pushed one leg under the falls, still holding onto a large boulder next to me. I felt around with my foot, making sure there was a solid surface where I could stand.

I stood up and simply walked under the waterfall.

I was standing in a cave behind the falls, looking out through a wall of water. It was beautiful.

"Are you all right?" I heard Susan yell, trying to be heard above the rush of water.

I thrust my arm out through the waterfall, waved, and then pulled my arm back inside. I slowly walked to the other side of the cave behind the falls, pushed my head through the water and looked for a place to step onto the far bank. I could see a narrow path behind a large boulder that kept it hidden from the other side of the stream.

I pulled my head back inside, took a breath and then just walked out from under the falls and onto the path. It was easy.

I climbed up onto the boulder and waved to Susan twenty feet away. I grinned, water dripping from me.

She didn't even hesitate. She walked through the waterfall and then, just a few seconds later, stepped onto the narrow path behind me.

"Wow," said Susan, shaking her hair. "That was amazing."

"There's a path here, too," I said. "Kirk McKenna has a secret. Our stakeout wasn't quite so ridiculous, was it?"

"No," said Susan. "Let's go."

We followed the twisting path. It ended in a small clearing. You couldn't see the clearing from the pond. It was hidden by a small ridge and by rocks and trees.

A shed stood in the middle of the tiny meadow.

Susan and I looked at each other, shocked. The wood for the shed must have been shipped to the village on a barge and then hauled up the path and carried under the waterfall. Kirk McKenna couldn't have built that shed without half the village helping him.

Kirk McKenna had a secret, but he wasn't the only one.

"How come none of the adults have ever told us it was possible to walk under the falls and that there was a shed up here?" I asked.

"Maybe," said Susan slowly, "maybe New Auckland is like one of the villages where all of the adults keep some terrible truth from the innocent children."

I laughed. I don't think my laugh sounded like a laugh from a person who was amused. It sounded like a laugh from a person who was at least slightly scared.

"Wasn't that the plot of some movie we saw recently?" I asked. "The one where all the villagers were aliens and the houses were holograms."

"But this shed is real. This shed is standing on the side of a mountain in the middle of the woods just above our village and it's a little bit too weird for me."

We walked around the shed to see if we could peek inside. There were no windows and the only door was padlocked. The walls were made from wide, rough pine boards that had turned gray with age.

The shed was taller in the front so that any rain water that hit the roof would fall away from the door. The roof was made from cedar shingles.

"Wait," I said, suddenly looking around.

"What?"

"Kirk McKenna must have a partner or a lot of partners. They might be out there in the woods watching us."

We both crouched low, our eyes darting around the meadow, looking for flashes of light off a binocular lens or a rifle barrel pointed in our direction.

I stopped and tapped Susan on the shoulder.

"Don't do that," she hissed. "You scared me."

"Maybe," I said quietly, "Kirk's partners are hiding inside the shed."

"They're not inside," said Susan.

"How do you know?"

"The door is padlocked on the outside."

"Then maybe," I said softly, "somebody is

locked inside, trapped. Remember those screams we heard?"

I backed up about ten paces and took a couple of deep breaths.

"What are you doing?" asked Susan.

"Being a hero," I said seriously as I ran at the door, shoulder first.

I bounced off the door and fell onto the ground.

"Maybe you're being an idiot," said Susan, shaking her head.

I stood up, rubbing my shoulder, and we each pressed an ear against the wooden door. If somebody was locked inside they might not be able to talk but they'd at least be able to rattle their chains or kick the wall.

"Anybody there?" I asked loudly.

"I don't think so," said Susan after about ten seconds.

"We have to be sure," I said firmly. "There may be a lock on the door but the hinges have screws. If we brush away our footprints we can come back with a screwdriver and open that door easily."

"Secrets," Susan muttered to herself as she stepped away from the shed and looked for a pine bough to use as a broom so that she could wipe away our footprints. "I wonder if keeping secrets makes a person so full of lies that they just have to spit."

7

Black Bear Hump

W^E borrowed Annie Pritchard's dinghy after school on Tuesday. It had a 25 horsepower outboard motor.

Annie Pritchard used it when she searched the shore for scenes to paint. Annie was one of the most famous painters in the world, but she lived in the same-sized house as everyone else in New Auckland. She was starting to get old and sometimes I would pilot her dinghy for her when she went puttering along the shoreline of the bay.

When Susan and I were close to shore near the narrows, I pulled up the motor so the propellers wouldn't bang against any rocks. The gentle waves pushed us toward the beach. Susan hopped out in ankle-deep water, grabbed the forward line and pulled us ashore. She tied the line around a rock. I hopped out and tied off the stern line.

"What do you think of our new teacher?" asked Susan as we started to look around.

We both wore shorts and old plastic sandals.

"Have you ever seen anything as funny as when that curl fell off?" I asked, laughing.

"Yeah," said Susan. "The sight of her gluing it back in place."

"I think we need to check on her. Let's face it. People who aren't born here don't usually move here when they're adults. If they do, they don't stay."

"Your dad did."

"Yeah, after Mom died, Dad ran away from any thing and any place that reminded him of her. But you're right. Dad came here because he was running from something and maybe Ms. Weatherly is running, too. But maybe she's running away from big thugs or tall men with wide shoulders who carry badges. Look at her. She wears a wig and thick make-up. She's probably trying to disguise herself."

"That's just crazy, Thumb. If she was going to wear a disguise don't you think she'd use a wig made from real hair instead of that bathing-cap thing?"

"Ah. But maybe that's part of her brilliance. You know what we should do?" I asked as we both walked along the beach with our heads down, looking for another cannonball or maybe a musket or a sword or a half-buried treasure chest.

"No. But I am willing to bet that whatever you say we should do is something that we most definitely should not do."

"We should try to peek inside her purse and see if maybe she has ID in some other name or a small gun or a stack of counterfeit hundred-dollar bills."

"Look up," said Susan.

"What?" I asked, ducking in case whatever I was supposed to see when I looked up was something coming down fast.

"Just look up."

I looked up, checking the sky. Nothing seemed to be falling, so I looked at the cliff above us and was surprised to see the trunk of a lone cedar tree jutting out from the top of the cliff.

"Hey," I said. "We're right under Black Bear Hump."

"Yeah. And?"

I could tell by her voice that I was missing something. My eyes darted along the cliff face, searching for any other reason why my neck should continue to be bent back at an angle that didn't feel natural.

"Am I supposed to be seeing anything else?"

"Nope."

I stopped looking up and looked at Susan. I could tell from her expression that I was still missing something so I looked up again.

"There's nothing more to see," said Susan. "Try putting together what we know."

I looked at her again and sighed. "I know that I already have a teacher and my dad is a teacher, too. And I know that I would prefer it if my friends did not behave like they were teachers by trying to make me figure out the answers to questions when they already know the answers."

"I'll give you clues," said Susan. "Here are four facts that just might be related."

Susan held up two fingers and said, "Big Charlie found that cannonball on this beach, very close to where we're standing right now."

Susan held up another finger. "That cannonball was never fired from any cannon, and it didn't wash up on shore but it still got here somehow."

Susan held up four fingers. "Our village is located in a small bay with a narrow entrance to the ocean and our bay makes a great harbor. If it didn't, we wouldn't have a village."

Susan held up all fingers and the thumb on her left hand. "Black Bear Hump would be a good place for somebody to put a cannon if they wanted to protect the bay. And here's a bonus fact. If sailors were to lug a cannon and some cannonballs up to Black Bear Hump and one of those cannonballs fell over the side of the cliff, then it would probably land where we are standing right now."

Since we were already counting things, I did a little counting of my own. I did it very quickly and in my head.

There was one huge reason I liked to make

sure Susan was my partner when we did projects at school.

She was much, much smarter than I was.

Even though my sore neck still hadn't quite recovered, I leaned back and took a long look at the cliff above our heads.

"So you are suggesting that it is possible that Captain James Cook or one of those other explorers used Black Bear Hump as a natural fort to protect the harbor."

"That is exactly what I am suggesting."

"Good."

I turned around and started walking back to Annie's dinghy.

"That's it? Good?"

"Actually," I said, starting to untie the stern line, "great. We will definitely get an A on this assignment."

"This assignment?"

"Ms. Weatherly gave us an assignment and you did much more than simply search the beach. You came up with a theory. Who cares if it's right or wrong? It is a very, very good theory. We will both get an A."

"So you don't really care if Captain Cook had a gun placement above our village?"

"Not really. Besides, I need a nap if we're going to stake out the village again."

"Again?"

"Sure. Look what we discovered in just one night. Besides, it's kind of fun to spy on our village, isn't it?"

8

A Theory

I DIDN'T have to sneak out for our second night of staking out the village.

Mayor Semanov called an emergency meeting to be held right after dinner at his house. He said he wanted to write a letter about the fishing quotas. Dad had to go, even though he didn't fish, because he was good at writing letters.

Dad told me to go to bed after I did my homework. Instead, I arranged the pillows again so they looked like me and covered them with blankets and just walked out the front door, meeting Susan at the fire truck.

"Our bad guy might not do anything tonight," I said to Susan. "There's a meeting at the mayor's house."

"Look," said Susan softly.

I turned and looked where she was pointing. Ms. Weatherly was walking toward the school, rolling a suitcase behind her.

We ducked down but kept watching as she opened the door to the school and walked down the short hallway to her classroom.

Susan and I slipped out of the fire truck and moved around the school building so that we could peek through a window and see what she was doing.

Ms. Weatherly had turned on the lights in our classroom and was pulling folded posters and books from her suitcase. The blinds were half closed and we couldn't see her very well.

We leaned against a huge rock, far away from the light of the window.

"Let's leave," whispered Susan.

"Why? We're supposed to be spying on people."

"Would you like it if somebody was sitting outside your house watching you wash dishes or read a book?"

"Why would anybody want to watch me read a book?"

"Exactly. And why should we want to watch our teacher put up posters in our classroom?"

"We're trying to learn about her. It's what spies do."

"Then let's go inside and help her. We can ask her questions. We'll learn more than we will by crouching out here in the dark."

Susan leaped up and started walking. I followed her.

"We can't," I said, just as Susan was reaching for the doorknob.

"Why not?"

"Because Dad thinks I'm at home studying and then going to bed. If she tells him we helped, he'll know I sneaked out."

"Good point," said Susan. "Let's go to Mayor Semanov's and tell our parents that we saw Ms. Weatherly walking to school and we're going to help her decorate."

She turned and started walking just as quickly toward the village.

"Why are we going to help her?" I asked, catching up with her.

"Because I feel really guilty about spying on her. It wasn't nice. And we're going to make up for it by being nice." She stopped and looked at me. "You are going to be nice, too, Thumb."

"Yes," I said meekly to Susan's back. She hadn't waited for an answer.

Susan reached Mayor Semanov's house first. She made a fist and held it close to the door, ready to knock. We could hear Mayor Semanov talking, and what he was saying made Susan freeze, her fist still raised. She lifted that fist to her mouth and raised one finger, motioning me to be quiet.

"What?" I whispered, stopping beside her.

"Listen."

I didn't have to put my ear close to the door. Mayor Semanov was talking loudly, and I could tell, right away, that the crowd in the mayor's living room wasn't talking about fish quotas at all.

"For fifteen years you've kept that shed secret, Kirk. How can you be so sure that somebody has been sneaking around?"

"Somebody tried to wipe away their footprints."

"Well, we certainly don't want your secret getting out."

"Why not?" asked Kirk McKenna. "I'm tired of hiding out in the woods. Is what I do really so bad?"

"Yes," sounded a chorus of voices around the room.

"It's evil," somebody said angrily.

"Horrible," said Dad. "Although maybe it's not so bad if you're Scottish."

Susan and I turned and looked at each other, puzzled.

And then, well, I couldn't help it. I guess I'd just eaten too fast so that I could get outside for the stakeout.

I burped.

It wasn't a soft, gentle burp, either. It was loud. Susan's eyes got big and we both realized that the voices in Mayor Semanov's living room were suddenly silent.

Susan and I raced around the corner of Mayor Semanov's house just as his front door flew open. I took the corner too widely and crashed into the house next door. My elbow hit glass and I heard a window crack and then shatter. I didn't stop. Susan and I ran across the sand and slipped into the fire truck, breathing hard.

"I don't think anybody saw us," I said.

"We'd better stay here, just to be safe."

"What if our parents look for us in our rooms?"

"We need an alibi," said Susan.

"Ms. Weatherly?"

"Yeah," said Susan. "Did I hear a window break?"

"It was an accident. I broke Annie's kitchen window."

"Oh, no."

Susan and I looked around to see if anyone was searching for us. We couldn't see anybody so we sneaked into the school and closed the door.

"Hello," Susan yelled loudly enough so that Ms. Weatherly would know we were there.

"Hello?" yelled Ms. Weatherly. We could hear her walk across the hardwood floors of our classroom and then saw her peek down the dark hall toward us. We waved.

"Thumb," said Ms. Weatherly, surprised, "and Susan, right?"

"We noticed that the lights in your room were on," said Susan, "and thought we'd see who was here."

"It's just me," said Ms. Weatherly.

"Can we tell you what we found out about the beach where Mayor Semanov found that cannonball?" I asked.

"Now? It can wait until the morning, you know."

"It's pretty interesting."

She hesitated for a moment and then sighed.

"Come on down," she said without much enthusiasm.

Susan and I walked down the dark hall. Ms. Weatherly stood beside her door.

She wasn't wearing so much make-up, and I could see she was much, much older than we had thought.

I gasped.

"You thought I was younger, didn't you, Thumb?"

I couldn't think of anything to say. I was good at lying when I could plan, like with my thumb, but not when I was surprised.

Luckily, Ms. Weatherly didn't wait for me to answer.

"The last school where I worked had a policy that people over a certain age had to retire," said Ms. Weatherly. "I retired. Not happily, though. I hate golf. I can't stand gardening. I don't want to learn bridge or any other stupid card game. New

Auckland was desperate for a teacher, and I was desperate to teach. So, here I am."

"You're here because you're desperate?" asked Susan.

"Yes. But it seems like a nice place."

"Sure," muttered Susan. "No bad people here."

"What?" asked Ms. Weatherly.

"Nothing. You can look as old as you want here," I said. "Nobody cares."

Susan kicked me, hard.

"I mean that people don't much care what clothes anybody wears. That's one good thing about the place." I grinned and added, "And if you really hate golf, then you don't have to worry about anybody begging you to play."

Ms. Weatherly laughed.

"Good point," she agreed. "So, what can you tell me about the cannonball?"

"We have a theory," said Susan.

And we told her.

9

Lots of Bad Guys

WHEN we had finished decorating the classroom, Ms. Weatherly and Susan and I all walked to my house.

Dad must have heard our voices because he threw open the door before we'd even arrived and shouted, "Where have you been?"

"Thumb and Susan were with me," said Ms. Weatherly. "They were helping me set up my classroom. Is there a problem?"

Dad looked up at her, startled, and then he looked up and down the sidewalk and motioned for us to get inside.

Dad closed the door behind us and then did something I had never seen done in any house in New Auckland.

He locked the door.

I had forgotten that our door even had a lock and had no idea how I would get it open if

I came home and discovered that the door was locked. I had never seen a key.

"There's something odd going on in the village," said Dad quietly.

"Odd?" asked Ms. Weatherly as we all sat down. I was glad that she was there and talking because my mouth was suddenly dry. I tried to look serious and folded my arms in front of me.

Dad suddenly looked more closely at Ms. Weatherly, surprised because she wasn't wearing make-up.

He stammered for a few seconds, trying to remember what he wanted to say.

"She's old," I said to Dad.

"Thumb!"

Ms. Weatherly laughed.

"He's right," she said. "I wore all that make-up so I wouldn't look so old but if I kept wearing it then the weight alone will make the loose skin on my face slide down my neck."

"It rains too much here anyway," I said.

Dad and Susan and Ms. Weatherly looked at me, confused.

"Unless your make-up is waterproof," I added.

"Enough," said Dad. "Besides, I have to tell you what happened tonight. We think somebody is vandalizing the village. Somebody broke the window in Annie's kitchen."

I tried to look confused.

Dad thought for a moment and then said, "I have to tell you, Ms. Weatherly, that one of the great thrills of living here is that people look out for each other. But now that's changed. It has changed over the past few days."

"The past few days," said Susan slowly. "There have been other incidents?"

Dad didn't seem to hear her. He was staring at Ms. Weatherly.

"Have you been up to the pond yet?" Dad asked her suspiciously.

Susan looked at me, wide-eyed. We both knew that Dad was wondering if Ms. Weatherly was the one doing all the spying.

"The pond?" she asked.

"It's where we get our drinking water."

"How do you get there?"

"There's a path," said Dad slowly, "out behind the school."

"Is that the same path that leads to Black Bear Hump?" asked Ms. Weatherly.

"How did you know about Black Bear Hump?" asked Dad, even more suspicious.

"Thumb and Susan told me about it tonight. They have a theory about that cannonball in front of the mayor's house."

"Cannonball?"

"Yes. It's an eighteenth-century cannonball."

"And Susan and Thumb were both with you tonight?"

"Yes," said Ms. Weatherly. "They have a theory about that cannonball. It's a good theory."

Dad sighed and sat down heavily in his favorite chair. He was convinced that Ms. Weatherly was too old to be walking under waterfalls.

I felt this sudden chill as I realized that Dad knew about that path under the waterfall, and he knew about Kirk McKenna's shed, too.

Susan grabbed my hand and squeezed. She was thinking the very same thing.

10

Another Stakeout

M s. Weatherly asked Susan and me to tell our theory to the entire class on Wednesday morning.

Neither of us had much energy and I couldn't even look at Susan. We had been looking for bad guys and now, somehow, we had either become the bad guys or we were the good guys in a village full of bad guys. I couldn't imagine my dad or any other adults, except maybe Kirk McKenna, being bad, but they were all hiding some horrible secret about that shed.

"So," said Susan, facing the class, "we went to the beach and kept wondering how a cannonball could have come to rest right there. I happened to look up and, Thumb, you tell the rest."

I told how we could see the cedar tree that leaned over the edge of the clearing at Black

Bear Hump and how Susan had the idea that maybe Black Bear Hump had been used as a gun placement to protect a ship that might have stayed in the bay while the crew did some repairs.

"And if Susan and Thumb's theory proves to be correct," added Ms. Weatherly, "then Captain Cook or Dixon or Vancouver and his men used Black Bear Hump as a gun placement and sailors slept up there at night. We might be able to prove this theory. There may be artifacts. We'll set up a search and take a look."

Susan and I both nodded and sat down. I don't know if Susan looked at me. I was trying very hard not to look at her.

The morning seemed to last forever but the bell finally rang for recess. Susan was already outside when I reached the door. She was down on the beach, skipping stones across the water.

Susan was the best stone skipper in the village. She might have been the best stone skipper in the world. She'd had enough practice. She had a large bay and an entire beach filled with flat skipping stones.

I slowly walked over and watched her pick up a few more stones and sidearm them across the surface of the water.

"Susan," I said, almost in a whisper.

She didn't answer. She picked up another stone and skipped it, too.

"Susan," I said again. "They think we're the bad guys. I mean, not really us because they don't know we're the ones sneaking around and breaking windows. But they think there is a bad guy."

"You're right," said Susan quietly. "Isn't it cool?"

"Cool?"

"Yeah. You were right. Bad guys add excitement to life. My dad was more excited than I've ever seen him this morning. You wanted excitement and now there is excitement. We're the excitement. Your plan worked. Just not quite the way you expected."

"But, they're going to figure out that we're the ones doing everything pretty soon."

"How?"

"We have to tell them."

"Are you nuts, Thumb?"

"If we don't, then everybody will be under suspicion. Besides, we haven't done anything wrong. We can explain."

Susan just stared at me, waiting for me to figure out something she obviously knew but I was too stupid to even consider.

"What?"

"You're going to tell them that we followed Kirk McKenna because we thought he was a bad guy?"

"No. We can tell them we saw a footprint and discovered the trail under the waterfall and found the shed. They'll believe us."

"You're forgetting one thing, Thumb."

"What?"

"We don't know what's inside that shed and we don't know why the adults are keeping it a secret from us. I'm not willing to tell anyone until we find out."

"I will not believe that my dad and your dad are bad guys, Susan."

Susan shrugged and tossed another stone. We both watched it skip and both silently counted to ourselves. Eight.

"How often do you think Kirk McKenna goes up to that shed?" I asked quietly.

"I don't know."

"Are you ready for one more stakeout?"

"Tonight?"

"No. Let's assume Kirk McKenna goes up there every Friday night."

"Friday night?"

"You bet."

11

Digging for Treasure

ON Wednesday Ms. Weatherly led the entire class up to Black Bear Hump.

She was puffing pretty hard by the time we reached the pond. I tried not to look at the waterfall and the stream that led out of the pond, but I did glance. It seemed almost impossible for me to have missed seeing how you could get to the other side.

I looked over at Susan. She frowned and shook her head.

There wasn't enough room at Black Bear Hump for all of us to stand in the small clearing, much less dig. Some of us, including Susan and me, sat on rocks and watched and listened to Ms. Weatherly talk about Captain Cook and Captain Vancouver and why they might have stayed in our bay when they searched along our coast for water routes inland.

While she talked, Big Bette and Little Liam divided the clearing into squares with yellow yarn stretched between stakes. Ms. Weatherly said that archeologists did that to keep track of where they dug.

Robbie and his dad had made a wooden box that looked like a drawer with a screen where the bottom should have been. While some of us dug, others sifted dirt through the screen, looking for artifacts.

"What will we find?" asked Big Bette, stopping for a moment to stretch her back.

"Probably nothing," said Ms. Weatherly. "It's only a possibility that one of those explorers had a cannon placement here but even if he did, there may not be anything left behind."

"But what might we find?"

"I don't know. Coins. Broken bits of the ceramic pipes that sailors used when they smoked. Buttons. It's doubtful that we'll find anything, but if we do, it could be evidence of the first Europeans to ever visit this part of the world."

"Wow," several kids whispered.

I was watching Little Liam and Big Bette as they started to dig. It looked like a lot of work so I held up my hand.

"Yes, Thumb?" asked Ms. Weatherly.

"I don't think I can take a turn digging," I said, trying to sound disappointed.

"Why?" asked Ms. Weatherly. I glanced around and could see Liam and Susan rolling their eyes.

"It's my thumb," I said, holding up my real thumb, the thumb that Ms. Weatherly thought was a fake. "Lifting a shovel full of dirt might put too much pressure on the delicate mechanism inside my thumb and it might break. It's pretty expensive. I'm supposed to be careful."

I tried to look disappointed.

Big Charlie's son, Little Charlie, was the first person in our village to pretend to have a fake thumb so that we could fool tourists. When he left the village to work back east, I was asked to pretend I had a fake thumb because I could keep a straight face and look innocent when I lied.

"Can you shift dirt?" asked Ms. Weatherly.

"I guess so," I said, leaving some doubt in case shifting dirt turned out to be a hard job.

Little Liam carried a chunk of dirt over to the drawer with a screen bottom and dumped the dirt inside. I picked up the drawer and shook it so the sandy dirt would rain through the bottom and anything bigger would stay inside. When the dirt was gone all that was left on the bottom of the drawer were pebbles and rocks and twigs. I dumped them onto the dirt pile and then kicked everything over the edge of the cliff, down to the rocky beach below.

My classmates took turns shoveling and sifting and kicking, but we didn't find anything that wasn't supposed to be there. It didn't feel like we were doing school work but Ms. Weatherly did talk the entire time, explaining how archeologists worked.

I was glad there was no stakeout that night. I was exhausted, even if I didn't have to shovel dirt.

We did an hour of math the next morning before heading back up the mountain, dragging shovels. We didn't walk quite as fast. We were all tired, and searching for treasure didn't seem so exciting any more. All we were doing was moving dirt.

In movies, when the heroes are about to be surprised, you can always tell because the music gets faster and more tense. In life, there is no music. In life, surprise comes suddenly, without warning.

Susan found the pewter ring right after lunch. It was simple in design and not very well made, but clearly from another century.

With eighteen kids crowded around her, Ms. Weatherly cleaned the ring with an old toothbrush and then slipped it onto her hand so that it wouldn't be lost. She made her hand into a fist so it couldn't possibly slip off and then, to be even more certain of not losing it, she held her fist up in the air.

We all stared at that raised fist with the pewter ring as we made our way back down Linda Evers Mountain to the village below. We walked faster, and not just because we were going downhill.

Ms. Weatherly walked right into the school

and into my father's classroom. The rest of us followed and spread out around the walls, surrounding the surprised primary grades at their desks.

Dad looked at all of us, mystified.

Ms. Weatherly waited until we were all inside and everyone could see and hear. Then, still holding her hand up high, she marched over to my dad, who was sitting at his desk, and she opened her hand right in front of his face and said, "Look!"

"Look at what?" asked Dad.

"Look at what we found up on Black Bear Hump. We found this ring. Susan and Thumb were right."

Dad stared at the ring and then slowly stood up.

"Excuse us, class," he said. "Ms. Weatherly and I have to make a phone call."

12

Caught!

IT wasn't hard for me or for Susan to escape on Friday night. We each just threw on a jacket and walked out our front doors. Our parents were at the gym with most of the other adults. Dad told me that they were meeting about the ring that Susan had found. A professor of archeology from the University of British Columbia was planning to fly up to see the site and the ring. If she said that what we had found was what we thought, then a team of twenty students and professors would soon be digging up at Black Bear Hump.

We didn't know where they would stay — probably on a research vessel that would anchor in the bay. It was all pretty exciting.

Susan and I knew that one of the few adults who wasn't at the gym was Kirk McKenna. We'd walked past his house and heard him inside, muttering. I could hear him spit a couple of times and wondered if he spat on the floor in his own house or if he had little containers all over the place so one was always close.

When we got to the fire truck, Susan and I crouched low inside the cab and stayed quiet.

It wasn't long before we saw the beam of a flashlight coming toward us. We ducked even lower, until we couldn't see and couldn't be seen. We heard soft footsteps on the sand.

The person holding the flashlight marched right past us. I lifted my head and saw the flashlight beam disappear on the other side of the boulder that hid the path up to our pond.

Susan and I didn't even look at each other. We climbed out of the fire truck and raced across the sand. We could see the flashlight beam twist around rocks and we quickly followed, being as quiet as we could.

We were following much more closely this time, confident that Kirk McKenna wouldn't suddenly turn around and find us. We knew where he was going. We just didn't know why.

We would. Soon.

We stopped behind the last boulder before the pond and peeked around the corner. We saw Kirk McKenna humming a Scottish tune to himself as he scooted down to the stream. He plunged through the waterfall below the pond and, a few seconds later, emerged on the other side. His flashlight meandered through the woods beyond the pond and then disappeared.

Susan and I scurried down to the waterfall and then behind it to the other side. We weaved through trees and around rocks, helped by a full moon. We could see the meadow and shed and could heard Kirk McKenna working a key in the padlock that held the door shut.

Kirk McKenna slid the opened padlock out of the clasp and swung the door open with a rusty screech. He stood in the doorway shining the flashlight beam onto shelves before pulling down a propane lantern and lighting it. Then he stepped inside and closed the door behind him.

Susan and I dropped to the ground and started to crawl slowly toward the shed.

Suddenly, we heard a horrible scream. It

was coming from inside the shed. Susan and I stood up, fast, but before I could decide if I was going to run toward the shed or away from it, somebody grabbed my shirt and my arm and yelled, "Got ya!"

I quickly looked over at Susan. Another large shape was holding her.

We'd been caught.

"March," the voice behind me ordered. I started walking toward the shed.

Flashlights suddenly appeared from all directions. Kirk McKenna opened the door to the shed and stood with his hands on his hips, grinning. He leaned outside, turned his head and spat down at the ground.

"So," he said, "we were pretty sure you were the ones who have been spying on me."

I didn't say anything. Neither did Susan. I don't think either one of us could have said anything. We were too scared.

I could see inside the shed now. I didn't see anyone tied up to a chair. I did see a wall lined with deep shelves like you'd see in a warehouse. On each shelf sat four or five black boxes. Each box looked like a small pirate's chest with the lid kept in place by silver clasps.

"I guess you're wondering what I've been hiding up here?"

"Maybe… a little," said Susan.

"Well, I'm going to show you," said Kirk McKenna with a lopsided sneer.

"Don't," pleaded a voice behind me. "They may have been spying but that doesn't mean they deserve to be tortured. Nobody deserves to be exposed to your madness."

Kirk McKenna didn't pay any attention. He reached back into the shed and picked up one of the black cases. He carried it over to a large flat boulder and set it on top. Flashlight beams shifted to focus on the case. The arms around me tightened and pushed me closer to the boulder.

I couldn't help but remember the movies we'd seen where the bad guys only showed the good guys their secret plans when they knew the good guys wouldn't live to tell.

I gulped as Kirk McKenna grinned at Susan and me. He started humming and opened the lid.

At first, all I could see was a long black barrel, like a rifle.

Then I noticed several other barrels and a cloth bag that attached the barrels together.

"Bagpipes?" I said, more to myself than to anyone else. Almost like an echo I heard Susan ask the same question.

"Yeah," said Kirk McKenna proudly. "I collect bagpipes. I play them, too, but I usually play inside the shed. The sound of the waterfall keeps anyone in the village from hearing."

He slowly looked around at the people behind the flashlights and sneered.

"They won't let me play my music down in the village."

"He's not that good," said the man who was holding me. I recognized his voice. It was Susan's dad. "And I don't like bagpipes even when they're played by a professional. They do have professional bagpipe players, don't they?"

"Of course, they do," said my dad, letting go of Susan. "But Kirk McKenna sure isn't one of them."

"You... you all knew about these bagpipes?" I stuttered.

"Sure," said Dad.

"Why didn't you tell us?" asked Susan.

"We don't tell any of the kids," said Mayor Semanov. "When kids are young we don't want them trying to walk under the waterfall. It's too dangerous. And when they're older we don't want them deciding that they like the sound of bagpipes."

"Like that's going to happen," said my dad with a chuckle.

"Would you like to hear me play?" asked Kirk McKenna. I had never seen him smile without sneering. He had a dimple on one cheek. It made him look a little less fierce.

"No!" shouted Dad and Mayor Semanov and other voices hidden behind flashlights.

"It was worth a try," said Kirk McKenna.

Mayor Semanov patted Kirk on the shoulder.

"No," he said. "It wasn't."

"We knew you and Susan had been here," said Dad. "We found your footprints. It wasn't hard to figure out they were your prints. They match your shoes."

"Why didn't you tell us?" asked Susan.

Dad shrugged.

"It was kind of obvious that you and Thumb were sneaking around and having fun, so we decided just to see what you'd do next. Hey, it was fun for us, too. We liked following you and trying to figure out just what in the world you were doing. And, Thumb, since you put pillows in your bed and climbed out the window, you will be punished."

"We knew you'd be hiding in that fire truck tonight so we told you we had to go to a meeting and came up earlier and waited for you," added Mayor Semanov. "Kirk led you right to us. We had fun being sneaky, right?"

"Right," echoed voices around us.

"Doesn't anyone want to hear me play the bagpipes?" asked Kirk McKenna.

"Actually," said Susan. "I do."

"Me, too," I said.

So Kirk McKenna led us into his shed and closed the door so that the sounds he made wouldn't drift down to the village and across the bay and scare kids or call wolves or confuse the sonar systems in whales and submarines under the ocean.

Susan and I learned something very important that night. We learned that even though no bad guys lived in New Auckland, British Columbia, one very bad bagpipe player did.

13

Belonging

THE town meeting had been called so that everyone could hear more about what we had found on Black Bear Hump.

The provincial museum would be sending up a crew of archeologists to dig for evidence that New Auckland was the earliest known site of any European artifacts on the north coast. Our village would be famous.

Mayor Semanov was already trying to figure out where the tourists would sleep and how much they might pay for food and souvenirs and guided tours and pictures taken with the cannonball that had sat on the sand in front of his house for years, ignored. He'd built a small hut around it, like a doghouse, so that it wasn't exposed to the sun and the rain.

There was another reason for the meeting, of course.

It was a chance for me to pretend to take off my thumb for Ms. Weatherly and then wiggle my real thumb and scare her in front of the entire village.

People had been stopping her on the sidewalk and grinning and shaking her hand and telling her that they wouldn't dream of missing such an exciting morning. She'd even been told that the fishing boats would stay in the harbor so that all of the fishermen could attend.

She did not know that the reason everyone was so excited was not so that they could celebrate our remarkable discovery, but so that they could see her reaction when my thumb, lying in a bed of cotton inside the beautiful wooden box that Annie Pritchard had carved for this very purpose, wiggled.

I have to confess that while I had a nickname that I liked far more than my real name, I didn't always like wiggling my thumb and scaring people. I particularly didn't like it when the person who was being fooled was a nice person like Ms. Weatherly, who was also my teacher and who would be giving me a grade at the end of the school year.

I dressed in my favorite shirt and pants and combed my hair a little more than usual. Then I slipped Annie Pritchard's wooden box into my jacket pocket and made my way to the gym.

The bleachers were filled. People smiled at me and winked. I waved and sat by Susan near the front.

Dad came over and nodded toward the door. I looked. Kirk McKenna stood at his usual spot, but he was wearing a kilt and long plaid socks and a dark jacket with a plaid shawl over one shoulder. The hat on his head looked like a flat, burnt pancake.

He seemed a little less grumpy as he turned his head and spat. A black suitcase with silver clasps rested close to his feet.

Dad leaned over and whispered, "We decided you were right. Kirk McKenna shouldn't have to hide in the woods. We're going to let him play."

I was sort of disappointed. Susan and I had solved a mystery and been told a secret that only the adults shared. Now everyone would know.

Dad nodded at Kirk and then walked to the middle of the gym so he could sit beside our mayor behind a table.

Kirk McKenna quickly put together his favorite bagpipe, blew air into the bag and marched into the gym, playing. He finished and smiled at the audience. Nobody asked for an encore but he left grinning.

After everyone had recovered their hearing, Dad and Mayor Semanov motioned for Ms. Weatherly to join them.

Ms. Weatherly was wearing a dark blue dress, and she carried a purse. I don't think I had ever seen anyone carry a purse before, at least not in New Auckland. She had decided not to wear make-up but she still wore her wig with the tight nylon curls. Big Charlie stood up and held out a chair for her.

She sat down, and Big Charlie cleared his voice and began.

"Thank all of you for coming. We are here, of course, to honor our new teacher, Ms. Weatherly. She discovered something about our village that we had never noticed. Sometimes, when you live in a place and pass by objects every day, you just don't question what they are or why they are where they happen to be. Ms. Weatherly," said Big Charlie Semanov, our sometimes mayor, "thank you."

Big Charlie started to clap and everyone in the bleachers clapped, too.

Ms. Weatherly blushed and, at Big Charlie's urging, she stood up to say a few words.

"Thank you all," she said, wiping a tear from her cheek. "I must say that I have enjoyed my short time here in New Auckland. It is one of the most beautiful places I have ever seen and you people have been so nice. You seem to have everything."

"Except a doctor," broke in Big Charlie. "Although we can get good medical care pretty quickly. I mean, they didn't manage to sew Thumb's thumb back on but they did manage to stuff it and put some tiny screws in the side. It looks almost real. Has Thumb taken it off for you yet?"

I thought he was being a little too obvious, but Ms. Weatherly didn't seem to notice.

"No," she said. "Not yet."

"Well, come on down here, Thumb, and show Ms. Weatherly that medical miracle, your very re-attached thumb which you can definitely and without question or doubt remove."

People clapped again, for me this time, and I could see my friends and neighbors start to lean forward.

Big Bette never could manage to keep a straight face whenever I was about to pretend to take off my thumb. I glanced at her. She was trying to hide her grin behind a book. Her eyes, filled with excitement, peered over the top.

I walked down to the table and stood beside it, facing the audience. Ms. Weatherly stood beside me. I wiggled my thumb for her and then pulled Annie's wooden box out of my pocket. I put the box in my other hand and reached back inside my pocket for a small screwdriver. The screwdriver was part of the act.

"I'm a little shy about taking my thumb off in front of people," I muttered and then turned my back to Ms. Weatherly and the crowd.

I knew that Big Charlie would be moving

into position. He always tried to stand behind my victims so he could catch them if they fainted.

I pretended to screw off my thumb and then I put the screwdriver back into my pocket. I slid my perfectly good and perfectly attached thumb into the hole at the bottom of the wooden box and then up and onto the cotton where it was supposed to rest. I adjusted the cotton and then closed the lid to the box.

Holding the wooden box in both hands, I sighed, fixed a smile on my face and then turned around again, showing Ms. Weatherly and the audience the wooden box in my hands.

"I'll open the box," I said softly. And I did.

Ms. Weatherly looked inside. She moved her head a little closer, trying to get a better look.

When she'd had a good long look, I wiggled my thumb.

I'd wiggled my thumb for maybe twenty visitors to our village. Most screamed. One fainted. Two just laughed. One backed off the dock and fell into the bay. Three sort of looked puzzled. One grinned and said, "Do that again."

Until Ms. Weatherly I had never had anyone stand up straight, scream and then pull hair out of her wig. Actually, Ms. Weatherly probably didn't pull. She just ran her hands along the sides of her head and dozens of tiny nylon curls fell to the floor.

Instead of catching Ms. Weatherly, Mayor Semanov tried to catch her curls.

Ms. Weatherly stopped screaming and looked back at Big Charlie. She glanced at her hands, each of which was full of blonde ringlets.

"I never lost my thumb," I told her quietly. "It's just a dumb joke."

Ms. Weatherly looked at me and then at the curls in her hand, mystified. I knew she wouldn't stay mystified for much longer, a few seconds at most.

For the first time, I was ashamed of being Thumb. Ms. Weatherly had done something good for the whole village and we ruined it by embarrassing her. I felt like a groom at a wedding who decides to wear one of those bow ties that lights up and twirls.

It just wasn't a very good idea.

I liked Ms. Weatherly. She was a good

teacher. And now she'd probably leave on the Thursday plane.

"So, taking off your thumb is like some kind of initiation rite?" asked Ms. Weatherly, turning to look at the entire audience. People had stopped laughing and just looked at her. I could tell by their faces that they didn't want her to be hurt or embarrassed. They liked her.

"It's exactly like an initiation rite," I said softly.

"And did I pass?" she asked, starting to smile.

"Definitely."

"Are there any more surprises?"

"Nope."

"So, I belong now?"

"Belong to what?"

"To the village."

"Yeah. You do."

"Then I'll stop wearing this stupid wig," Ms. Weatherly said as she pulled the bathing cap off her head. She had very short, very white hair. "Since I've passed your initiation rite, can I stay?" she asked loudly.

"Yes," everyone said together.

She bowed to the audience and said, loudly enough for everyone to hear, "Then you've got me."

People clapped and cheered more loudly than they had when she'd merely been introduced as a teacher who'd discovered something amazing.

Ms. Weatherly smiled, and I knew that she'd be our teacher for the rest of that year and for years to come and that, after she finally retired, she would stay.

She couldn't possibly leave.

She belonged.

KEN ROBERTS is the author of several popular books for young readers, including *Hiccup Champion of the World*, *Crazy Ideas*, *Pop Bottles*, *Nothing Wright*, *Past Tense* (shortlisted for a Governor General's Award) and two highly praised previous Thumb books — *The Thumb in the Box* and *Thumb on a Diamond*. Ken is chief librarian of the Hamilton Public Library and is currently president of the Canadian Library Association. He lives with his family near Brantford, Ontario.